TO:

_____

From:

_____

WORLD OF ERIC CARLE
An Imprint of Penguin Random House LLC, New York

To find out more about Eric Carle and his books, please visit eric-carle.com.
To learn about The Eric Carle Museum of Picture Book Art, please visit carlemuseum.org.

Visit us online at www.penguinrandomhouse.com.

ISBN 9781524790820

10 9 8 7 6 5 4

HAPPY BIRTHDAY

from The Very Hungry Caterpillar

world of
ERIC
CARLE

An Imprint of Penguin Random House

Today is **yOur** day!

You
are…

standing

tall...

climbing

high...

open your
presents...

dance with your
friends...

enjoy your
cake.

Today you will feel extra
special...

But always remember,
to me,

you're special
every day.